ZOM-AZING POSTERS, FACTS & MORE!

RANDOM HOUSE 🏠 NEW YORK

rhcbooks.com
ISBN 978-0-7364-3964-0
Designed by Diane Choi
Printed in the United States of America
10 9 8 7 6 5 4 3 2 1

© Disney

MEET ZED

- 15 years old
- Loves football
- Has a 7-year-old sister named Zoey
- He's a zombie—and proud of it!

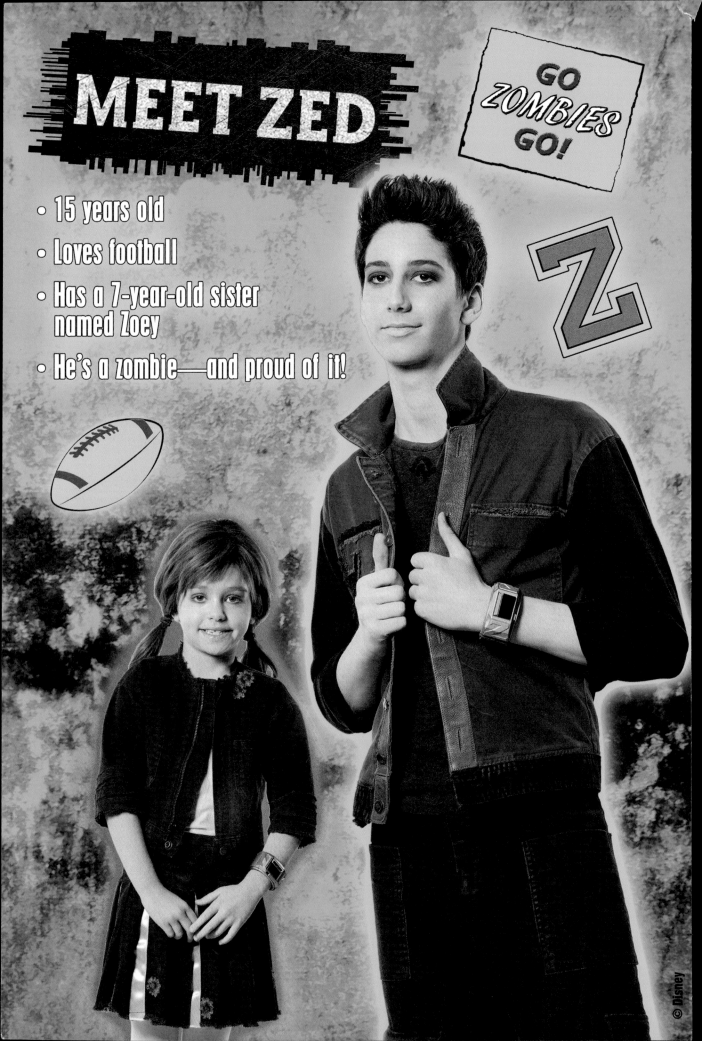

ZED

"I'm not a monster.
I'm a zombie!"

Meet Addison

SEABROOK

- 15 years old
- Loves cheerleading
- Wears a wig to cover her silvery-white hair
- Wants to fit in

ADDISON

"This is gonna be my year!"

SEABROOK HIGH SCHOOL

HOME OF THE MIGHTY SHRIMP

CHEER TIME!

MEET BUCKY

- A high school senior
- Head cheerleader
- Addison's cousin
- Loves winning and being the center of attention

BZFs: **BEST ZOMBIE FRIENDS**

~~No~~ ZOMBIES KNOW ZOMBIES

Where did the zombies come from?

Many years ago, a lime soda spill at the Seabrook Plant caused a green haze to spread. Anyone touched by the haze turned into a zombie!

Do these zombies eat brains?

Not anymore, thanks to the Z-Band they wear on their wrists. Soothing electromagnetic pulses from the Z-Band squash those brain-eating desires.

Why do the zombies' clothes all look similar?

They have to wear government-issued coveralls. But some zombies find ways to customize their clothes to show their individuality.

What's a zombie party called?

A zombie mash!

Can zombies party all night long?

No. They have a curfew.

Are zombies afraid of anything?

Yes. Fire.

Where do the zombies live?

They live in an area of Seabrook called Zombietown. A while back, zombies were forced to stay in Zombietown. But now they can go wherever they want—even to Seabrook High School!

ZED + ADDISON

Meet Bree

SEABROOK HIGH SCHOOL
SQUILLA FORTI SEMPER

- Loves glitter lip balm
- Makes the cheer squad as a stand-in
- Very talkative and always excited
- People call her "Babbly Bree" and "Bubbly Bree"

CHEERTASTIC!

BE FEARLESS

CHEERMATES

MEET BONZO

- Speaks in zombie tongue
- A classically trained musician
- A great artist
- Loves giving hugs

Meet Eliza

- 15 years old
- Into computers and technology
- Doesn't like humans
- Wants more rights for all zombies

BAMM!

"Cheer till it hurts!"
~Bucky

Bucky expects the best from his cheer squad. Anyone trying out for the team had to do just one move: a back-handspring-funky-chicken-round-off-mashed-potato-split, with a robot-powering-down finish. **Easy-peasy!**

SEABROOK

SHRIMP 13

EELS 28

DOWN 3

20 TO GO

ADDISON

"I'm cheering for change!"

© Disney

Zoey wants a real animal more than anything. Too bad zombies aren't allowed to have pets. (Some people think they'll eat them!)

Zombie siblings rule!

Be Fearless
Not Cheerless!

ZOMBIE CHIC

Zombies use their creativity and flair to change their government-issued clothes into one-of-a-kind designs.

Three Cheers for Bree!

I'M CRAZY!

I'M CUTE!

A ZOMBIE, TO BOOT!

Zoey likes to cheer too!

GET FIRED UP!

"Zombies don't do pep rallies."
~Eliza

© Disney

SPEAK ZOMBIE

chargzeer = cheer

hagrazug = hug

gruzik = music

Nagrazutty rargrazain stargrazick =
Thanks for rubbing peanut butter
on my umbrella

Plus there are
23 different words
for "brains"!

Addison's mom, Missy, is mayor of Seabrook.

Addison's dad, Dale, is chief Zombie Patrol officer.

Her family has hated zombies ever since one bit off her grandfather's ear!

Hi from Zombietown!

Before they become friends, Eliza refers to Addison as Perky Von Cheerstick and Little Miss Cheer-Boots.

ZOMS and POMS— PERFECT TOGETHER

© Disney

OOK

EELS

TO GO

Z

ZED

Eliza is not a fan of humans.
"Somebody crack a window. It stinks of human in here."

PALS IN PASTELS

NORMALS

ZOMBIES

GH SCHO